The Sign of a Friend

This story shows the value of learning new ways
to communicate with each other.

Story by:
Michelle Baron

Illustrated by:

David High	Lorann Downer
Russell Hicks	Rivka
Douglas McCarthy	Matthew Bates
Allyn Conley-Gorniak	Fay Whitemountain
Julie Ann Armstrong	Marilyn Gage

WORLDS OF WONDER™

Worlds of Wonder, Inc. is the exclusive licensee, manufacturer and distributor of The World of Teddy Ruxpin toys.
"The World of Teddy Ruxpin" and "Teddy Ruxpin" are trademarks of Alchemy II, Inc., Chatsworth, CA.
The symbol W•W and "Worlds of Wonder" are trademarks of Worlds of Wonder, Inc., Fremont, California.

Grubby™ Newton Gimmick™ Princess Aruzia™ Leota™ Wooly What's-It™ Prince Arin™ Fobs®

Teddy

Talking is pretty important, isn't it?

Grubby

I agree...especially because of what happened to me once. Hey, Teddy, why don't ya tell everyone about that?

Teddy

Alright, Grubby, that's a good idea.

Grubby

Thanks. Ya know, even though somethin' kinda bad happened to me, it ended up okay. Remember?

Teddy

I sure do, Grubby.

It was a beautiful day, and Newton Gimmick had invited Grubby and me to join him on a nature hike in the forest. Gimmick told us the names of all the different plants we passed along the way.

Page 1

Gimmick

This delicate foliage is "stepticoniconi pigmatoliosus." Its crimson leaves produce a most effective red dye.

Teddy

It looks just like the red in your tablecloth.

Gimmick

Very observant, Teddy. I used the leaves of this plant to color the tablecloth.

Grubby

Gee, that's fascinatin', Gimmick.

Teddy

Yes, it is.

Gimmick

Oh, and here's some aromatic "tastioni zestofini."

Grubby

Zestahoochi tootsifruitsi?

Gimmick

Tastioni zestofini. It's an herb…a spice.
I add it to all my soup broths.

Grubby

Oh boy, I love your soups, Gimmick; and
just sayin' tostimosti zippydooda makes
my mouth water.

Gimmick

Well, it's lucky that we came this
way because we're low on tasti…
"soup weed." Would you fellas help
me pick some?

Teddy

Of course, Gimmick.

Grubby

I'll tell ya one thing. Talkin' about
plants is sure a lot harder than
eatin' 'em.

Teddy

While we were picking the "soup weed," I noticed a most unusual looking plant right next to it.

What is this plant?

Gimmick

I'm so glad you asked me about it, because this is a strange plant with a pretty strange name...the "shush-bush."

Teddy

The "shush-bush?"

Grubby

"Shush-bush?" Well, it sure does taste good.

Gimmick

Oh no, Grubby, don't eat that!

Grubby

Huh?

Teddy

Gimmick what's wrong?

Gimmick

Ohhh...I didn't have the chance to explain. The "shush-bush" is called the "shush-bush" because it has been known to cause a temporary paralysis of the larynx mechanism.

Teddy

What does that mean?

Gimmick

It means Grubby could lose his voice!

Grubby

That's silly. These cute little shush-berries are too good tastin' to be bad for ya. In fact, I feel better than I did when...

Teddy

What did you say, Grubby?

Gimmick

You see? You see? It's working...or it's not working! I mean the plant's working, and Grubby's voice is not!

Teddy

Are you sure? Grubby, say something! You're right, Gimmick. Grubby's lost his voice! Look Gimmick, Grubby's trying to tell us something.

Teddy

Grubby was moving his arms about, first one way, then the other. We tried hard to figure out what he was trying to say, but we couldn't understand.

Gimmick

You want to play an accordion?

Teddy

You're thirsty, and you want a bucket of water?

Gimmick

No, no, I got it! You want to play Grungeball!!

Teddy

I don't think that's what he means, Gimmick. I know! Gimmick, do you have a pencil with you...

Gimmick

Of course.

Teddy

...and some paper?

Gimmick

I always do.

Teddy

Okay, that's great. Grubby, you can
write down what you're trying to tell us.
Here, Grubby.

Teddy

H...O...W...L...O...N...G..., how...long!

Gimmick

How long? How long is the accordion?

Teddy

No, I don't think so, Gimmick. I think Grubby wants to know how long this will last.

Gimmick

Oh, it's been known to last anywhere from one hour to ten years!

Teddy

Grubby started running around in circles and waving his arms about every which way. Then he calmed down. Grubby didn't have to write down what he was trying to say this time. We could see that he was pretty upset.

I know it'll be hard to write all the time, Grubby, but it seems the best way to understand you.

Teddy

Oh, look! There's Leota!

Leota

Hi, fellas! How are you today?

Teddy

Oh, Leota, Grubby ate some of that "shush-bush" over there...

Leota

Oh my!

Teddy

...and now he can't talk.

Leota

Oh, poor Grubby, I hope you've learned that you shouldn't eat things if you don't know what they are.

Teddy

Grubby nodded his head up and down to say "yes."

Leota

Now you're trying to figure out a way to talk with your friends, right?

Teddy

Yes, Leota, we figured out that Grubby could write down what he wants to say to us. Right, Grubby? See, Leota?

Leota

Yes, and writing things down is a very good idea; but I have an even better way for Grubby to talk with you...

Teddy

How?

Leota

...with his hands.

Gimmick

With his hands?!

Leota

Sure, it's called Sign Language. It's the language that deaf people use to talk. You see, deaf people have problems hearing, and sometimes when they speak, they don't sound the way we do. So deaf people use their hands to talk.

Teddy

Oh, you mean when I point my finger at something I want, or wave "hello" to Grubby, I'm using Sign Language?

Leota

Well, not exactly, Teddy. You're talking about "gestures," and using gestures is one very good way to talk without using your voice. But Sign Language is different. It's a real language. Anything you want to say out loud you can say, sometimes even more beautifully, with your hands.

Teddy

That sounds great, Leota. How does it work?

Leota

Like this!

Leota

Place one of your hands on top of the other hand, palms touching.

Teddy

Okay. Got it. Grubby does, too.

Leota

Now slide the top hand all the way across.

Gimmick

Like this?

Leota

Yes, that's right. You just made the sign for "nice."

Gimmick

I did?

Teddy

"Nice"...hey, this is fun!

Leota

Now point both index fingers straight up in the air...and let your hands bump. You just signed "meet."

It's nice

to meet

Teddy

"Meet"...this is great!

Leota

Now, to say "you" just point to another person.

Gimmick

Oh, this one's easy.

Teddy

"You."

Leota

Now put them all together, and we can say *and* sign, "It's nice to meet you."

Teddy & Gimmick

It's nice...to meet...you!

Leota

Very good, you got it. Now follow me...

you.

It's a beautiful

day

"It's Nice to Meet You"

Chorus:
It's nice to meet you.
It's nice to meet you.
It's a beautiful day.
It's a beautiful day.
It's nice to meet you.
It's nice to meet you.
Come on and play.
Come on and play.

It's nice to meet you.
It's nice to meet you.
I'm feeling fine.
I'm feeling fine.
It's nice to meet you.
It's nice to meet you.
I'm glad you are
   a friend of mine.
I'm glad you are
   a friend of mine.

come on and

play.

It's easy to say, "It's a beautiful day."
Curve your fingers around right in front
   of your nose.
Then pointing your finger up at the sun,
Down it goes.

Repeat Chorus

It's simple to say, "Come on and play."
Just wave at a friend till he comes right
   to you,
Then make a swing with your pinky
   and thumb.
That's really all you have to do.

Repeat Chorus

I'm feeling fine.

I'm glad

I know you can sign, "I'm feeling fine."
With your hand opened wide,
Touch your thumb to your chest.
Now there's one more thing you must
    learn to say,
The thing I like saying the best...
I'm glad you're a friend of mine.

you are

a friend of mine.

I'M GLAD...
Now pat your chest while moving your
hands up because your heart is light.
YOU ARE...
Point at your friend.
A FRIEND...
Lock your index fingers together to
show friendship
OF MINE.
Place your hand on your chest.

Repeat Chorus

Teddy

That was really fun. How did you learn to do all that, Leota?

Leota

One of the students in my class taught me. Her name is Katie. Katie is deaf. You know, before I learned Sign Language, I couldn't talk with Katie very well.

Teddy

Well, I wouldn't like to think that there was someone in the world I couldn't talk to.

Leota

Oh, I understand how you feel, Teddy. That's why all the students in my class learned to sign. Not only can we say things in beautiful new ways, but most importantly, we can talk with Katie.

Teddy

Wouldn't it be wonderful if everyone learned Sign Language?

Leota

Oh, it sure would, Teddy.

Teddy

Gee, Leota, I'd like to meet Katie. And I think Grubby would, too.

Gimmick

Yes, so would I.

Teddy

But how do we tell her our names?

Leota

You spell them. You can make every letter of the alphabet with just one hand, like this. It's called "fingerspelling."

Teddy

Leota spelled each of our names with her hands. Then she gave each of us a very special sign that only meant *our* names! She called it our "name sign."

Leota

I think we'll make Gimmick's name sign the letter "G" on his head because he's really smart.

Gimmick

Oh, thank you.

Leota

You're welcome. And Grubby's name sign will be a "G" on his tummy because he loves to eat. And Teddy's name sign will be a "T" right by his heart because he's a true friend.

Teddy

Thank you, Leota. Now we can introduce ourselves to Katie.

Leota

That's right. Say, why don't you all come to school tomorrow? It'll be a nice surprise for the students.

Teddy

We'll be there, Leota.

Leota

Tonight I'll bring you a book with all kinds of signs in it. You can practice and learn a lot of signs.

Teddy

Gee, that'll be great, Leota.

Teddy

That night Leota brought us a wonderful book. It had lots of colorful pictures about signing. Grubby was working hard and learning new signs as fast as he could.

Gimmick

Teddy, look at Grubby. He's making three signs at one time! What's he saying?

Teddy

"I'm hungry now." Gee, Grubby, with all those hands you can sign a whole sentence at once! Tomorrow you'll be the fastest signer of all! What was that, Grubby? Oh, I see what you're saying. "Enough talk. Let's eat!"

We sat down to dinner in our usual way, but we did something different. We closed our mouths and only talked with our hands. The only time we opened our mouths was to eat! The next morning, Grubby was the first one out the door. As we walked we practiced more Sign Language, and soon we arrived at Leota's school.

I'm

hungry

now.

Leota

Hello! Students, it seems that we have some visitors. Would you like to introduce yourselves to the class?

Teddy

Well, Grubby quickly began fingerspelling our names and then told them our name signs. The students were really surprised!

Students

Look he's signing! Wow! He's signing! Oh, Sign Language! Wow!

Teddy

Then, one by one, they started introducing themselves to us in Sign Language, until finally we met Katie.

Teddy

Gimmick signed…

Gimmick

Very pleased to know you, Katie.

Teddy

…and I signed, "It's nice to meet you, Katie,"…and Grubby signed, "I'm glad to meet you, Katie." Then Katie signed to us, "It's nice to meet you, too. Wow! You sign very well!"

Gimmick

Thank you.

Teddy

Yes, thank you, Katie.

Grubby

Yeah…it's lots of fun.

Teddy

Grubby! Grubby! You got your voice back!

Grubby

I did? Testing…one, two, three. Hey, Teddy, you're right! I did! But ya know, even though I lost my voice, I never stopped talkin'.

…very well.

Thank you.

Leota

Now, Grubby, remember Sign Language is just one way to talk without saying a word.

Gimmick

You're right, Leota. Why you can also say, "It's nice to meet you" by just shaking someone's hand.

Grubby

Or when ya pat me on the back when I'm feeling bad, Teddy, that always makes me feel better.

Teddy

Aw, Grubby, you know a pat on the back, a handshake, or even a smile are ways in which we can all talk without saying anything. They're all special signs of a friend.

"The Signs of a Friend"

There are some signs that we
  all understand.
I know what it means when you're holding
  my hand.
The way that I smile when I see you again.
These are the many signs of a friend.

There is a sign that I use to say "hi."
It's the same sign that I use for "good-bye."

I wink my eye when I wanna pretend.
These are the many signs of a friend.

The sign of a friend doesn't have to
  be heard.
You can say "friend" without saying
  a word.

Lock fingers together with some of
    your friends,
And make a circle that never ends.

There are some signs that are a must;
Signs of affection, of friendship and trust.
If you need a sign, I have one to lend.
There are so many signs of a friend.

The sign of a friend is so easy to see.
You can say "friend" just by bein' with me.
The power of friendship is there in
    your hands,
So let's make a sign everyone understands.

There are some signs that are a must;
Signs of affection, of friendship and trust.
If you need a sign, well I have one to lend.
There are so many...
So very many...
There are so many signs of a friend.